W9-DDF-526

Welcome to ALADDIN QUIX!

If you are looking for fast, fun-to-read stories with colorful characters, lots of kid-friendly humor, easy-to-follow action, entertaining story lines, and lively illustrations, then **ALADDIN QUIX** is for you!

But wait, there's more!

If you're also looking for stories with tables of contents; word lists; about-the-book questions; 64, 80, or 96 pages; short chapters; short paragraphs; and large fonts, then **ALADDIN QUIX** is *definitely* for you!

ALADDIN QUIX: The next step between ready to reads and longer, more challenging chapter books, for readers five to eight years old.

Read more ALADDIN QUIX books!

By Stephanie Calmenson

Our Principal Is a Frog!

Our Principal Is a Wolf!

Our Principal's in His Underwear!

Our Principal Breaks a Spell!

Our Principal's Wacky Wishes!

A Miss Mallard Mystery
By Robert Quackenbush

Dig to Disaster

Texas Trail to Calamity

Express Train to Trouble

Stairway to Doom

Bicycle to Treachery

Gondola to Danger

Surfboard to Peril

Taxi to Intrigue

Cable Car to Catastrophe

Dogsled to Dread

Stage Door to Terror

Rickshaw to Horror

THE GIANTS' FARM

THE
GIANTS' FARM

BY
Jane Yolen

ILLUSTRATIONS BY
Tomie dePaola

ALADDIN QUIX

New York London Toronto Sydney New Delhi

ALADDIN QUIX

Simon & Schuster Children's Publishing Division

1230 Avenue of the Americas, New York, New York 10020

First Aladdin QUIX hardcover edition February 2023

Text copyright © 1977 by Jane Yolen

Illustrations copyright © 1977 by Tomie dePaola

Also available in an Aladdin QUIX paperback edition.

All rights reserved, including the right of reproduction in whole or in part in any form.

ALADDIN and the related marks and colophon are registered trademarks of Simon & Schuster, Inc.

For information about special discounts for bulk purchases, please contact Simon & Schuster Special Sales at 1-866-506-1949 or business@simonandschuster.com.

The Simon & Schuster Speakers Bureau can bring authors to your live event. For more information or to book an event contact the Simon & Schuster Speakers Bureau at 1-866-248-3049 or visit our website at www.simonspeakers.com.

Designed by Karin Paprocki

The text of this book was set in Archer Medium.

Manufactured in the United States of America 1222 LAK

2 4 6 8 10 9 7 5 3 1

Library of Congress Control Number 2021948590

ISBN 9781534488588 (hc)

ISBN 9781534488571 (pbk)

ISBN 9781534488595 (ebook)

For Heidi E. Y. Stemple and Peter B. Tacy,

who make me happy and give me room

and time to write

—J. Y.

Cast of Characters

Grizzle: the biggest giant

Dazzle: the roundest giant

Grab: Grub's twin

Grub: Grab's twin

Little Dab: the smallest giant

Contents

Chapter 1: The Farm   1

Chapter 2: The Secret   10

Chapter 3: Dazzle's Candy   20

Chapter 4: Grizzle's Grumble   30

Chapter 5: And Little Dab   42

Recipe   59

Word List   63

Questions   67

1

The Farm

Long ago there were five giants who wanted to live together on a farm.

There was **Grizzle**. He was the **biggest** and liked to build things.

Dazzle was the roundest, and she loved to cook.

The twins—**Grab** and **Grub**—always stuck together.

Last was the little giant **Dab**, who loved to read.

To make the farm, first the giants had to clear the land. Grizzle picked up **huge boulders**. He laid them one on top of another to make an **enormous** wall.

Together, Grab and Grub moved trees whose bark looked like long, **shaggy** dresses.

Dab read a book that showed her how to rake everything smooth.

And Dazzle, as usual, made something for everyone to eat. **YUM!**

Next, they had to build a **mammoth** house of wood. It had to be just the right size for five **enormous** giants.

Grab and Grub sawed the **beams**.

OOF!

Grizzle put on the roof.

Dab gave out the nails.

And Dazzle, as usual, made something delicious for everyone to eat.

Then the giants brought in stuff for the house—things just the right size for giants.

Grizzle brought in a **great** grandfather clock and a **tremendous** couch and chairs.

Grab and Grub moved in a grand piano with keys the size of hockey sticks.

Little Dab carried in **big** books and **bigger** bookcases.

And Dazzle made the yummy
dinner as usual, using the pots and
pans she had packed with care.

At last they sat down to eat, and

Dab said, "Now that we have a farm, what shall we call it?"

"How about George?" said Grizzle.

Little Dab sighed. "Not poetic enough."

"How about Our Home?" asked the twins.

"Too plain," said Dab.

"Pudding Place?" Dazzle asked, licking her lips.

No one paid any attention to that. Instead they all **growled** at little Dab. "What do *you* like best?"

"I don't know," said little Dab.

"But it will come to me. Such things take a little time."

In the middle of dinner, Dab looked up and smiled. "I know the best name for a giants' place." She raised her mug of flower water.

"To Fe-Fi-Fo-Farm!" she said.

"YAY!" they all agreed.

And so their farm was named.

The Secret

Now that the farm was named, the giants had other problems to worry about. Some they shared, but some they did not.

It turned out, Grab and Grub had a secret. **A BIG secret.** Of course, when any other giant had a secret, they kept it . . . well . . . secret!

One giant, one secret.

But Grab and Grub were twins. They were so much alike, they were like one person.

If Grab was happy, Grub was happy.

If Grub was sad, Grab was sad. And when one of them had a secret, they *both* had a secret.

And this one was **mega**-secret. They **swore** to each other that they would not tell.

It was a serious swear.

A promise.

An oath.

Grab ran to the place where Grizzle was building a table. Grizzle was pounding in a nail.

"We have a secret," Grab said.

Grizzle growled and hammered in another nail. "So—what is your secret?"

"We won't tell," said Grab.

The nail went in with a **large** pound of the hammer. **_WHACK!_**

The nail squeaked, and the table **trembled.** But it did not fall apart.

At the same time, Grub had gone into the kitchen, where Dazzle was standing over a **HUGE** pot on the floor.

"We have a secret," Grub said.

Dazzle frowned and ate a melon.

"What is your secret?" she asked.

"We won't tell," said Grub. **"It's a SECRET!"**

Dazzle sighed, turned away, and ate another melon.

So, together, Grab and Grub ran up to the little giant Dab. "We have a secret," they said.

Dab looked up from her book. "I
cannot hear you," she said.

Grab shouted, **"We have a . . ."**
And Grub added, **"Secret!"**

Dab put her hand to her ear, then
whispered, "I am the smallest giant.
I have the smallest ears. Small ears

cannot hear small sounds. I cannot hear what you are trying to tell me."

Grab looked at Grub. Grub looked at Grab. "We are not telling you anything," they said. "It is our secret, and we will *not* tell you."

"I cannot hear you with my little ears," said Dab. She looked down at her book and began to read.

Grab ran to one side. Grub ran to the other. They each whispered in one of Dab's little ears. "We will not tell you that today is our birthday," they said, "because it is a secret."

Dab put down her book and took the twins by their hands. **"Happy birthday!"** she whispered.

"How did you guess that was our secret?" asked the twins. But they seemed very pleased that little Dab knew about it.

Dab smiled. "I'll never tell."

3

Dazzle's Candy

After Grub left with his secret **untold**, Dazzle realized she wanted something sweet to eat. But today the cookie jar was empty.

"I will have to make it myself," she said. "I will have to make something truly sweet to eat."

She took out a bowl. Then she opened a cookbook. It had been her grandmother's cookbook, and it was **HUGE**. Even **MONUMENTAL**! It was called *The BIG Book of Sweets*, and she knew it was a great choice.

Carefully, she turned to the "Best Candies for Secrets" page, and there was a recipe for **Giant** No-Cook Bonbons. Dazzle smiled to herself.

"No one will ever know that these bonbons were not cooked," she whispered to herself, "so I will have a secret too."

The picture of bonbons in the book made her hungry. She looked at the recipe.

2 tbsp. butter
1/8 tsp. vanilla
10 tbsp. confectioner's sugar
3/4 c. chopped nuts

Dazzle scratched her head. "I do not know where to get these things," she said. "I do not know what a 'tbsp.' is. I do not know what a 'tsp.'

is. I have never heard of a 'c.'"

She sat down at the table and cried **great big** tears, as **big** as raindrops, that each fell off her nose and dropped into the bowl with a loud ***KERPLOP!*** Soon the bowl was full and even **overflowing** with tears.

Dab came into the kitchen. "What are you doing?" she asked.

"I am making something sweet to eat," Dazzle said with a **sniff**.

"It looks as if you are making something to drink," Dab said with a kind smile.

"I want to make **Giant** No-Cook Bonbons," said Dazzle. "But I cannot do it." She pointed to the book.

Dab read the recipe. "Do we have butter?"

"Yes," said Dazzle.

"And do we have the right kind of sugar?" asked Dab.

"Yes," said Dazzle.

"Do we have vanilla and nuts?" asked Dab.

"Yes and yes," said Dazzle.

"Then what is possibly wrong?"

Dazzle began to sniff again. "I do not have a 'tbsp.' or a 'tsp.' or a 'c.,'" she said. "*That's* what's wrong."

Dab tilted her head to one side.

"A 'tbsp.' or a 'tsp.' or a 'c.'?"

"Yes," Dazzle said, pointing to the page. "And there they are, all in a row!"

Dab began to laugh. It was not a nasty laugh. It was a nice laugh. "I will show you what those are," she said.

She took a pencil and wrote in the book:

Giant No-Cook Bon-bons

TABLESPOONS
2 tbsp. butter

teaspoon
1/8 tsp. vanilla

TABLESPOONS
10 tbsp. confectioner's sugar

CUP
3/4 C. chopped nuts

"Oh!" said Dazzle, a **huge** smile on her face. "I know what those are!"

Dazzle followed the revised recipe. In an hour she was done. She was so pleased with how the bon-bons turned out, she invited the other giants to share her candy after dinner.

The twins said, "The candy is delicious. How did you know it was our birthday? **That was our secret!**"

Dazzle was **confused.**

She looked at Grizzle.

Grizzle was confused. He looked
at Dab.

"Oh," said Dab, "I bet a little bird
told her."

Dazzle looked outside. All the birds were in their nests except for one very large owl sitting on a **limb** of the closest tree.

"Or maybe," Dazzle added, "a very **big** one." And she pointed to the owl.

"That must be it!" the twins agreed, laughing loudly.

At the sound of their laughter, the owl flew away.

4

Grizzle's Grumble

The next day was a gray and drizzly day. All the giants were stuck at home.

Grizzle began to grumble. No

one was listening to him, so he
grumbled louder.

Still no one heard. So at last he began to sing a **big** grumbling song:

*"I do not like being **big**.*
*I do not like being **big**.*
I fall and break things,
then have to remake things.
*I do not like being **big**."*

This time, some of the other giants heard him.

"You are right," said Dazzle. "It's no fun being **big**. A **big** hand gets caught in the cookie jar."

This made Grizzle even sadder. He sang his grumble loudly!

*"I do not like being **big**.*
*I do not like being **big**.*
Nothing fits right.
Nothing sits right.
*I do not like being **big**."*

"You are right," said Grab.

"You are right," said Grub.

Then Grab added, "If you are **big**, you get all the hand-me-ups. Like the socks that have lost all their elastic."

And Grub added, "Plus sweaters that are all stretched out."

Grizzle felt worse and worse. His chin fell to his chest. His mouth turned down. Two **great big** tears started in his eyes. He tried to sing his grumble again, but it came out this way: "I do not ... *blub* ... *blub* ... *blub*."

Little Dab came into the room. "I have a **big** problem."

"I have a **big** problem too," said Grizzle. "And it's me."

He began to "*blub … blub … blub*" again.

"My **big** problem is that I am not **big** enough," said Dab. "I cannot reach the book I want. It is on the very top shelf."

"I will get it," said Grab, but he could not reach that high.

"Then I will get it," said Grub, but he could not reach it either.

Dazzle wiped her mouth. "I would try to get it," she said. "But if Grab can't reach it and Grub cannot get it either, then I cannot."

"Oh dear," said Dab. **"This is a *bigger* problem than I thought!"**

Grizzle stopped blubbing. He got up, grabbed the book easily, and handed it to Dab.

Dab smiled up at him. "I don't know what I would do without some **really huge** friends around,"

she said. "I can solve the *little* problems. But for **big** ones, I need a **big** friend. In fact, I need an **enormous** friend, a **gargantuan** friend."

Grizzle thought about this for a while. Then he smiled a **great big** smile.

The sun came out, and it was no longer a gray day.

5

And Little Dab

But even good days, sunny days,
after a while can turn into cold,

even snowy days, and so it was at Fe-Fi-Fo-Farm. Snow fell for a day and a night, and no one could go out.

Grizzle slept. He dreamed and dreamed warm and wonderful dreams.

Dazzle cooked and cooked. She cooked delicious food for everyone.

Grab and Grub giggled and talked. They told each other terrific things: riddles, jokes, and rhymes.

But little Dab was bored. She looked out the window. All she could

see was cold snow, icy snow, lots
and lots and dots and pots of snow.

"I liked it in the spring," said
little Dab. "That was when we made
the farm and named the farm. We

planted our garden. I read lots of books. I liked it then."

"Zzzzzz," said Grizzle.

"I liked it a lot in the summer," said little Dab. "That was when we watered and **weeded** our garden. We watched it grow. I reread all the books while sitting under a tree. I liked it then."

"Munch!" said Dazzle.

"And I liked it in the fall," said little Dab. "That was when we picked vegetables and fruit from our garden, cooking and canning them to eat later. Then we made our garden ready for its long winter sleep. I read all the books a third time. I liked it then."

"Giggle-giggle," said Grab and Grub.

"Yes," said little Dab, looking out the window. "I liked it in the spring and summer and fall. I liked making something out of nothing.

I liked reading all the books three times. I was happy and grateful then.

But I have **memorized** every single book. There is nothing new to read. I do not like winter at all."

Grizzle opened one eye. "You need to dream," he said. "Winter is the right time for dreaming."

He closed his eyes and fell asleep again.

Dazzle stopped between bites. "You need to fill up with something sweet," she said to Dab. "Winter is the right time for that." She closed her mouth and kept on chewing.

Grab and Grub looked at each other. They giggled. "Make up riddles and jokes and rhymes," they said. "They always help us pass the time. And winter has plenty of time." They giggled again.

Little Dab turned away. She was very sad.

Each of the other giants had something to do through winter, something to keep them **focused** and fascinated. But Dab had nothing— except watching the snow.

One flake.

Two flakes.

They kept falling down.

After a little while, they were boring.

Little Dab thought about dream-ing. Then she thought about eating. She thought about making up things. She thought about sleeping and filling and telling. About making something from nothing.

"I'VE GOT IT!" Dab shouted into Grizzle's ear.

Grizzle kept on sleeping.

"I'VE GOT IT!" Dab shouted into Dazzle's open mouth. Dazzle kept on eating.

"I'VE GOT IT!" Dab sang in between Grab and Grub's giggles. They kept on playing.

Little Dab ran to the desk. She took out a piece of paper and a pencil.

She sat down by the window. She did not stare or glare at the snow. She hummed and grinned.

Grizzle sat up. Dazzle stopped eating. Grab and Grub forgot their

games. "What have you got?" they asked.

"I will show you," said little Dab. "It is a dream. It is filling and sweet. It is full of stories. And it will be easy to read."

Dab smoothed out the paper before her. She took up the pencil. She began to write:

LONG AGO, there were five giants who wanted to live together on a farm. . . .

And she wrote and wrote her own book, until spring found them once again.

Recipe

A recipe for you to make with a grown-up

Dazzle's GIANT No-Cook Bonbons

2 tablespoons butter

1/8 teaspoon vanilla

10 tablespoons confectioner's sugar

3/4 cup chopped nuts

Chocolate (sweet or dark—your choice)

1. Take the butter out of refrigerator.

2. Let it get soft.

3. Mash the butter with a spoon.

4. Keep mashing it. It will look like whipped cream.

5. Mix the vanilla in, one drop at a time.

6. Add the sugar, one spoonful at a time, to the butter-and-vanilla mixture.

7. Mix and mix and mix some more.

8. Add the chopped nuts a few nuts at a time.

9. Mix and mix and mix some more.

10. Take a large pinch of the mixture with your fingers.

11. Roll it into a ball. Take another, and make another.

12. Make twelve balls in all.

13. Line a plate with wax paper.

14. Put all the balls on the plate.

15. Put the plate and the candy balls in the refrigerator.

16. Let them get hard.

17. If you can, pour melted sweet chocolate over the candies. Then they will really be "bon-bon." That is French for "good, good."

18. Have a happy day, whether it is your birthday or not.

Word List

beams (BEEMZ): Long pieces of wood or metal used to build houses

boulders (BOWL•duhrs): Very large rocks

confused (kuhn•FEWSD): Not understanding what is being said

focused (FO•cussed): Paying attention to one thing or subject

gargantuan (ghar•GAN•chu•win): Very, very big in size

growled (GRAHW•uhld): Made an angry, low sound

limb (LIM): A branch of a tree

mammoth (MA•muth): Huge, big, gigantic in size

mega (MEH•gah): Very

memorized (MEH•moh•ryzd): To remember word for word

monumental (mawn•yu•MEN•tull): Very great in importance

overflowing (oh•vur•FLO•wing): So full that liquid spills over the top

shaggy (SHA•ghee): Like thick, tangled hair

sniff (SNIF): A short breath through the nose

swore (SWOHR): Made a promise

trembled (TREM•bulld): Shook

tremendous (truh•MEN•duss):
Huge, big, gigantic in size

untold (uhn•TOLD): Kept secret

weeded (WHEE•did): Pulled
weeds out of or cleaned out an
overgrown garden

Questions

1. What season does little Dab not like? Why does she like the other seasons better?
2. Why was Dazzle having trouble making the bonbons?
3. What do the giants name their farm? If you had a farm, what would you name it?
4. Who is the biggest giant? Who is the smallest?
5. Which giant likes to grumble the most?